Christmas Makes Me Think

written by **Tony Medina**

illustrated by **Chandra Cox**

LEE & LOW BOOKS Inc.

New York

Text copyright © 2001 by Tony Medina
Illustrations copyright © 2001 by Chandra Cox

LEE & LOW BOOKS Inc., 95 Madison Avenue, New York, NY 10016
leeandlow.com

Manufactured in China by South China Printing Co., March 2013
Book design by Tania Garcia
Book production by The Kids at Our House

The text is set in Journal.
The illustrations are rendered in cut paper, acrylic, pastel, and
colored pencil.

HC 10 9 8 7 6 5 4 3 2 1
PB 10 9 8 7 6 5 4 3 2
First Edition

Library of Congress Cataloging-in-Publication Data
Medina, Tony.
Christmas makes me think / by Tony Medina ;
illustrated by Chandra Cox.— 1st ed.
p. cm.
Summary: A young African American boy reflects on the spirit of Christmas and thinks
of ways he can share what he has with others.
ISBN 978-1-58430-024-3 (hc)   ISBN 978-1-60060-345-7 (pb)
[1. Christmas—Fiction. 2. Sharing—Fiction. 3. Christian life—Fiction.
4. African Americans—Fiction.] I. Cox, Chandra, ill. II. Title.
PZ7.M52537 Ch 2001
[E]—dc21   2001023428

For my father, Tony Medina, Sr., who paid for acting lessons, and didn't come down on me when I quit. It was on those cold Saturday morning subway rides from the Bronx to Times Square that I first encountered people who didn't have a place to live. That experience helped to propel my level of empathy.   —T.M.

To my mother and the memory of my father, Marjorie and James. And to my niece, Christa Janine, whose loving spirit brings joy to my life. I believe in you.   —C.C.

Christmas is coming!
Christmas is here!

It's my favorite time
when us kids get to have more fun
like watching cartoons at night
and no school 'til next year.

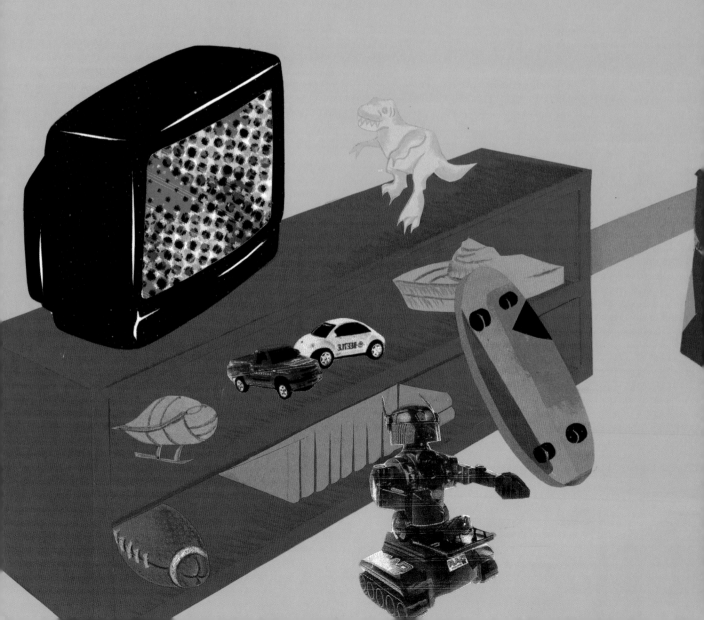

Christmas makes me think
about helping my grandmother
bake a chocolate cake
and getting to lick the spoon.

Christmas makes me think
about our big bright colorful tree
with lots and lots of lights
and presents piled to the moon.

But what about all those trees
that never make it
to the next Christmas?

How could we pray and sing and wish for nice good things when trees are chopped down for us to hang bulbs and lights on them?

TREES FOR S

Christmas makes me think
of how much better it would be
to just visit a tree and give it presents.

Or visit a turkey or a pig and instead
of eating one—feed it!

Christmas makes me think
about toys I have
but don't even play with
or clothes and shoes that I don't use.

What about all the people
who don't have a place to live
or food to eat or presents in a stocking
or under a tree?

Christmas makes me think
that I should share my presents
with kids who don't have any.
And get my friends to share too.

We could be like new Santas
giving homeless people hats
and gloves and scarves —
sharing hot soup and songs!

Because that's what Christmas
should be about
not just fancy toys
and the biggest tree.

Christmas is coming!
Christmas is here!
It's my favorite time—

I wish it could last and last
a week, a month, or even a year.

Christmas makes me think
about others
and not just me!

Ever since I was a kid, Christmas has been my favorite time of year. It was when my family and friends came together to share good times and good feelings—not to mention good food and presents! But as I got older, I realized that not everyone was as lucky as I was. Some people didn't get to eat, let alone receive presents. I wondered what I could do to make Christmas more special for those who were hungry and out in the cold.

I decided to get my friends and family together to collect food and clothing for the homeless in my neighborhood in Harlem. We stayed up all night cooking, until we could barely keep our eyes open. We fed over two hundred people, even whole families! People were so grateful to receive a home-cooked meal and free clothes. When we saw the smiles on their faces, we realized we really had made a difference.

Here are some suggested activities to help you get involved in your community. For many of these projects, you'll want to get the help of a parent or another adult. You don't have to limit yourself to these ideas. You can come up with your own ways to help others too!

- Find a soup kitchen and volunteer to serve food or help clean up.
- Make decorations and holiday cards to help lift someone's spirits.
- Hold a garage sale and donate the money you receive to a charity.
- Collect canned goods, toys, and clothing (especially cold-weather clothes) to donate to a local shelter or soup kitchen.
- Find a senior center near you and see if they take volunteer visitors—you could brighten someone's day!
- Ask your teacher to invite someone who does community service work to speak to your class. Then everyone can learn more about problems in the community and how to get involved.
- Organize a cleanup day in your neighborhood or school. Help to set up recycling stations and teach people about composting. —Tony Medina

FURTHER RESOURCES:

50 Simple Things Kids Can Do to Save the Earth, by The Earth Works Group (Andrews McMeel, 1990, 156 pages)

Homeless, by Bernard Wolf (Orchard Books, 1995, 48 pages)

It's Our World, Too!: Stories of Young People Who Are Making a Difference, by Philip Hoose (Little Brown & Co., 1993, 176 pages)

The Kid's Guide to Service Projects: Over 500 Service Ideas for Young People Who Want to Make a Difference, by Barbara A. Lewis (Free Spirit Publishing, 1995, 176 pages)

What a Load of Trash, by Steve Skidmore (The Millbrook Press, 1991, 40 pages)